A Sea-Wishing Day

Written by
Robert Heidbreder

Illustrated by
Kady MacDonald Denton

Kids Can Press

I wished so hard
To sail the sea
That the sea
Sailed right to me!

Around my toes
   Water splashed,
And Skipper's tail
   Thumped and thrashed.
"Matey — the sea,"
   He seemed to say.

"Let's hop a ship
    And sail away …
Where wild adventures
    Will abound,
Where golden treasure's
    Lost and found."

AHOY!
A ship came billowing by.
Aboard we sprang,
Skipper and I.

I shimmied the rigging
To the crow's nest.
I skimmed the deep blue
From east to west.

A rogue wave arose
Larboard ahead.
We'd capsize for sure!
Starboard we sped …

When up surged nine heads
Of a foul-smelling beast

With mean teethy mouths,
Ready to feast.

"LANDWARD!" I yelled —
  Nine heads blocked the sun —
"We won't be sea chowder
  For anyone!"

We ran aground
 On a coconut isle,
Where on the sand snored
 An old crocodile.

We skipped 'cross the croc
From stem to stern,

Then scouted the dark isle's
Each twisty turn …
Till I heard Skipper bark:

"A chest of gold!"
We dug it free,
Then both grabbed hold.

But up to the shore
A ship shot fast.
A black crossbones flag
Flew from its mast.

"PIRATES!" I shouted.
"We've stolen their chest.
Quick! Grab some driftwood.
We'll surf to the west."

Up popped a porpoise.
It offered a ride.
We bobbed through the drink
As it swam with the tide.

We braved the high seas,
Holding on hard
Till we spotted the tree
In our very own yard.

When we landed ashore,
The sea was gone.
There was only the pool
That sat on our lawn.

But Skipper and I,
    We've both been to sea,
So know the sea's near
    When you want it to be.

We've found there's real
    Treasure in sailing away
And wishing a ship
    On a sea-wishing day.

For the Ahrens family, friends in rough seas and fair — R.H.

For the pirates at Stony Lake — K.M.D.

Text © 2007 Robert Heidbreder
Illustrations © 2007 Kady MacDonald Denton

Kids Can Press acknowledges the financial support of the Government of Ontario, through the Ontario Media Development Corporation's Ontario Book Initiative; the Ontario Arts Council; the Canada Council for the Arts; and the Government of Canada, through the BPIDP, for our publishing activity.

Published in Canada by
Kids Can Press Ltd.
29 Birch Avenue
Toronto, ON M4V 1E2

Published in the U.S. by
Kids Can Press Ltd.
2250 Military Road
Tonawanda, NY 14150

www.kidscanpress.com

The artwork in this book was rendered in gouache. The text is set in Gill Sans.

Edited by Yvette Ghione and Tara Walker
Designed by Kady MacDonald Denton
Printed and bound in China

This book is smyth sewn casebound.

CM 07 0 9 8 7 6 5 4 3 2 1

Library and Archives Canada Cataloguing in Publication

Heidbreder, Robert
    A sea-wishing day / written by Robert Heidbreder ; illustrated by Kady MacDonald Denton.

ISBN-13: 978-1-55337-707-8
ISBN-10: 1-55337-707-9

1. Children's poetry, Canadian (English). I. Denton, Kady MacDonald II. Title.

PS8565.E42S39 2007   jC811'.54   C2006-902840-0

Kids Can Press is a C○rus™ Entertainment company

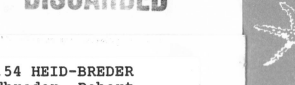